Joyce
Marx
Hardy
Defoe Abbott
Melville
Montaigne
Machiavelli
Haggard
Chesterton
Cooper
Emerson
Austen
Hugo
Eliot
Grimm
Stoker
Christie
Carroll
Wilde
Maupassant
Byron
Moliere
Schiller
Engels
Garnett
Goethe
Einstein
Fitzgerald
Hawthorne
Smith
Kafka
Cotton
Dostoyevsky
Kipling Doyle
Hall
Willis
Baum
Henry
Nietzsche
Leslie Dumas
Flaubert
Turgenev
Balzac
Stockton
Vatsyayana
Crane
Burroughs
Verne
Curtis Tocqueville
Vinci
Whitman
Gogol
Homer
Widger
Tolstoy
Busch
Darwin
Thoreau
Potter
Freud
Zola
Lawrence
Twain
Scott
Plato
Kant Jowett
Stevenson
Dickens
Harte
Andersen
Cervantes
Burton
Hesse
London
Descartes
Voltaire
Poe Aristotle
Wells
Cooke
Hale James
Hastings
Bunner
Shakespeare
Irving
Richter
Chekhov
Chambers
Dore
Dante
da
Shaw
Wodehouse
Benedict
Pushkin
Alcott
Swift
Newton

 **tredition®**

tredition was established in 2006 by Sandra Latusseck and Soenke Schulz. Based in Hamburg, Germany, tredition offers publishing solutions to authors and publishing houses, combined with world-wide distribution of printed and digital book content. tredition is uniquely positioned to enable authors and publishing houses to create books on their own terms and without conventional manu-facturing risks.

For more information please visit: www.tredition.com

TREDITION CLASSICS

This book is part of the TREDITION CLASSICS series. The creators of this series are united by passion for literature and driven by the intention of making all public domain books available in printed format again - worldwide. Most TREDITION CLASSICS titles have been out of print and off the bookstore shelves for decades. At tredition we believe that a great book never goes out of style and that its value is eternal. Several mostly non-profit literature projects provide content to tredition. To support their good work, tredition donates a portion of the proceeds from each sold copy. As a reader of a TREDITION CLASSICS book, you support our mission to save many of the amazing works of world literature from oblivion. See all available books at www.tredition.com.

Project Gutenberg

The content for this book has been graciously provided by Project Gutenberg. Project Gutenberg is a non-profit organization founded by Michael Hart in 1971 at the University of Illinois. The mission of Project Gutenberg is simple: To encourage the creation and distribution of eBooks. Project Gutenberg is the first and largest collection of public domain eBooks.

Psyche

Molière

Imprint

This book is part of TREDITION CLASSICS

Author: Molière
Cover design: Buchgut, Berlin – Germany

Publisher: tredition GmbH, Hamburg - Germany
ISBN: 978-3-8424-3015-0

www.tredition.com
www.tredition.de

Copyright:
The content of this book is sourced from the public domain.

The intention of the TREDITION CLASSICS series is to make world literature in the public domain available in printed format. Literary enthusiasts and organizations, such as Project Gutenberg, worldwide have scanned and digitally edited the original texts. tredition has subsequently formatted and redesigned the content into a modern reading layout. Therefore, we cannot guarantee the exact reproduction of the original format of a particular historic edition. Please also note that no modifications have been made to the spelling, therefore it may differ from the orthography used today.

PSYCHE.

BY

MOLIÈRE

TRANSLATED INTO ENGLISH PROSE.

WITH A SHORT INTRODUCTION AND EXPLANATORY NOTES.

BY CHARLES HERON WALL

'Psyche' is a *tragédie-ballet*. Molière had sketched the plan, written the prologue, the first act, and the first scenes of the second and third acts, when the King asked him to have the play finished before Lent. Pierre Corneille, then sixty years old, helped him, and wrote the other scenes in a fortnight. Quinault wrote the words of the songs.

Molière acted the part of Zephyr.

PERSONS REPRESENTED.

JUPITER.
VENUS.
LOVE.
ZEPHYR.
AEGIALE *and* PHAËNE, *two Graces.*
THE KING.
PSYCHE.
AGLAURA.
CIDIPPE.
CLEOMENES *and* AGENOR, *two princes,* PSYCHE'S *lovers.*
LYCAS, *captain of the guards.*
A RIVER GOD
TWO CUPIDS.

PROLOGUE.

The front of the stage represents a rustic spot, while at the back the sea can be seen in the distance.

SCENE I.

FLORA. *appears in the centre of the stage, attended by* VERTUMNUS, *god of trees and fruit, and by* PALEMON, *god of the streams. Each of these gods conducts a troup of divinities; one leads in his train* DRYADS *and* SYLVANS, *and the other* RIVER GODS *and* NAIADS.

FLORA *sings the following lines, to invite* VENUS *to descend upon earth:—*

FLORA.

The din of battle is stayed;
  The mightiest king of earth
His arms aside has laid;
  Of peace 'tis now the birth!

Descend thou, lovely Venus,
And blissful hours grant us!

VERTUMNUS *and* PALEMON, *and the divinities who attend them, join their voices to that of* FLORA, *and sing the following words.—*

CHORUS OF DIVINITIES *of the earth and streams, composed of* FLORA, NYMPHS, PALEMON, VERTUMNUS, SYLVANS, FAUNS, DRYADS, *and* NAIADS.

A peace profound we now enjoy,
And games and bliss without alloy;
Earth's mightiest king has giv'n us rest;
To him be praise and thanks addrest.
Descend thou, lovely Venus,
And happy hours grant us!

Then is formed an entry of the ballet, composed of two DRYADS, *four* SYLVANS, *two* RIVER GODS, *and two* NAIADS, *after which* VERTUMNUS *and* PALEMON *sing the following dialogue:—*

VERTUMNUS.
Yield, yield, ye beauties stern,
To sigh 'tis now your turn!

PALEMON.
See you, the queen above,
She comes to breathe soft love!

VERTUMNUS.
A fair one stern for aye
Ne'er wins a faithful sigh!

PALEMON.
To woo has beauty arms,
But gentleness has greater charms.

BOTH (*together*).
To woo has beauty arms;
But gentleness has greater charms.

VERTUMNUS.
Seek not your hearts to shield;
To pine is law, and ye must yield.

PALEMON.
Is aught more worthless born
Than hearts that love will scorn?

VERTUMNUS.
A fair one stern, for aye
Ne'er wins a faithful sigh!

PALEMON.
To woo has beauty arms,
But gentleness has greater charms.

BOTH (*together*).
To woo has beauty arms,
But gentleness has greater charms.

FLORA *answers the dialogue of* VERTUMNUS. *and* PALEMON. *by the following minuet, and the other divinities join their dances to the song.*

> Does wisdom say,
> In youth's heyday,
>   Sweet love forego?
> Be up, in haste
> These pleasures taste
>   Of earth below.
>
> Youth's wisdom too
> Is love to woo,
> And love to know.
> If love disarms,
> It is by charms;
> So yield your arms.
>
> 'Twere madness 'gainst his darts
> To seek to shield your hearts.
> Whate'er the bond
> Of lover fond,
> 'Tis sweeter chain
> Than freedom's gain.

Venus *descends from heaven, attended by* Cupid, *her son, and two Graces, called* Aegiale *and* Phaëne; *and the divinities of the earth and the streams once more unite their songs, and continue by their dances to show their joy at her approach.*

Chorus *of all the Divinities of the earth and the streams.*

A peace profound we now enjoy,
And games and bliss without alloy;
Earth's mightiest king has giv'n us rest;
To him be praise and thanks addrest.
Descend thou, lovely Venus,
And happy hours grant us.

Ven. (*in her chariot*). Cease, cease, all your songs of joy. Such rare honours do not belong to me, and the homage which in your consideration you now pay me ought to be reserved for lovelier charms. To pay your court to me is a custom indeed too old; everything has its turn, and Venus is no longer the fashion. There are rising charms to which now all carry their incense. Psyche, the beauteous Psyche, to-day has taken my place. Already now the whole world hastens to worship her, and it is too great a boon that, in the midst of my disgrace, I still find some one who stoops to honour me. Our deserts are not even fairly weighed together, but all are ready to abandon me; while of the numerous train of privileged graces, whose care and friendship followed me everywhere, I have now only two of the smaller ones who cling to me out of mere pity. I pray you, let these dark abodes lend their solitude to the anguish of my heart, and suffer me to hide my shame and grief in the midst of their gloom.

Flora *and the other deities withdraw; and* Venus *with her retinue descends from her chariot.*

SCENE II. — — VENUS, CUPID, AEGIALE, PHAËNE, CUPID

AEGI. We know not what to do, goddess; while we see you over-whelmed by this grief, our respect bids us be silent, our zeal would have us speak.

VEN. Speak; but if your cares would please me, leave all your advice for a fitter time; and speak of my wrath but to own me right; that was the keenest insult my divinity could ever receive; but revenge I shall have if gods have any power.

PHA. Your wisdom, your discernment, are greater than ours in deciding what may be worthy of you; yet, methinks, a mighty goddess should not thus give way to wrath.

VEN. That is the very reason of my extreme anger; the greater the brilliancy of my rank, the deeper the insult. If I did not stand on so lofty a height, the indignation of my heart would not be so violent. I, the daughter of the Thunderer, mother of the love-inspiring god; I, the sweetest yearning of heaven and earth, who received birth only to charm; I, who have seen everything that hath breath utter so many vows at my shrines, and by immortal rights have held the sovereign sway of beauty in all ages; I, whose eyes have forced two mighty gods to yield me the prize of beauty—I see my rights and my victory disputed by a wretched mortal. Shall the ridiculous excess of foolish obstinacy go so far as to oppose to me a little girl? Shall I constantly hear a rash verdict on the beauty of her features and of mine, and from the loftiest heaven where I shine shall I hear it said to the prejudiced world, "She is fairer than Venus"?

AEGI. This is the way with mortals, this is the style of mankind; they are impertinent in their comparisons.

PHA. In the century in which we live, they cannot praise without insulting great names.

VEN. Ah! how well does the insolent rigour of these words avenge Juno and Pallas, and comfort their hearts for the dazzling glory which the famous apple has won me. I see them rejoicing at my sorrow, assuming every moment a cruel smile, and with fixed gaze carefully seeking the confusion that lurks in my eyes. Their triumphant joy, when this affront is keenest felt, seems to tell me,

"Boast, Venus, boast, the charms of thy features; by the verdict of one man was the victory made over us, but by the judgment of all, a mere mortal snatches it from you." Ah! that blow is the direst; it pierces my heart, I cannot bear its unequalled severity; the pleasure of my rivals is too great an addition to my poignant grief. My son, if ever my feelings had any weight with you, if ever I have been dear to you, if you bear a heart that can share the resentment of a mother who loves you so tenderly, use here your utmost power to support my interests, and cause Psyche to feel the shafts of my revenge through your own darts. To render her miserable, choose the dart that will please me most, one of those in which lurks the keenest venom, and which you hurl in your wrath. See that she loves, even to madness, the basest and lowest of mortals, and let her hear the cruel torture of love unreturned.

CUP. In the world nothing is heard but complaints of Cupid; everywhere a thousand freaks are laid to my charge, and you could not believe the evil and the foolish things which are daily said of me. If, to assist your wrath ...

VEN. Be gone; no longer resist your mother's wishes; use reasoning only to find the shortest method of offering a sacrifice to my outraged glory. Let your departure be your only answer to my entreaties, and do not see my face again until you have avenged me.

CUPID *flies off, and* VENUS *withdraws with the two* GRACES. *The scenery changes to a large town, with palaces and houses of different architecture on both sides of the stage.*

ACT I

SCENE I. — — AGLAURA, CIDIPPE.

AGL. My sister, there are sorrows which are rendered greater by keeping them to ourselves; let us speak freely of our joint distress, and give vent in our conversations to the poignant grief which fills our hearts. We are sisters in misfortune, and your heart and mine have so much in common that we can unite them, and in our just complaints murmur, with a common lament, against the cruelty of our fate. My sister, what secret fatality makes the whole world bow before our younger sister's charms? and how is it that, amongst so many different princes who are brought by fortune to this place, not one has any love for us? What! must we see them on all sides pressing forward to lay their hearts at her feet, whilst they pass our charms slightingly by? What spell has heaven cast over our eyes? What have they done to the gods that they are thus left without homage amidst all the glorious tribute of which others proudly boast? Can there be for us, my sister, any greater trial than to see how all hearts disdain our beauty, and how the fortunate Psyche insolently reigns with full sway over the crowd of lovers who ever attend her?

CID. Ah! my sister, our fate is enough to bereave one of reason, and all the ills of nature are nothing in comparison.

AGL. At times I can almost shed tears over it; it takes away my happiness and my rest; my constancy finds itself powerless against such a misfortune; my mind is for ever dwelling over it, and the ill success of our charms and the triumph of Psyche are ever before my eyes. At night, unceasingly, comes to me the remembrance of it, and nothing can banish the cruel picture. As soon as sweet slumber comes to deliver me from it, it is immediately recalled to my memory by some dream which startles me from my sleep.

CID. That is just what I suffer from, my sister. All that you say, I see myself, and you depict everything that I experience.

AGL. Well, let us discuss the matter. What all-powerful charms have been bestowed upon her? Tell me how, by the least of her looks, she has acquired honour in the great art of pleasing? What is there in her person that can inspire such passion? What right of sway over all hearts has her beauty given her? She has some comeliness, some of the brilliancy of youth; we are all agreed upon that, and I do not gainsay it. But must we yield to her because we are her seniors by a few years? Must we, therefore, consider ourselves quite commonplace? Are we made so as to excite derision? Have we no charms, no power of pleasing, no complexion, no good eyes, no dignity and bearing, by which we may win hearts? Do me the favour, sister, to speak to me frankly. Am I, in your opinion, so fashioned that my merit is below hers? And do you think that she surpasses me in her attire?

CID. You, my sister? By no means. Yesterday, at the hunt, I compared you and her for a long time, and, without flattery, you appeared to me the more beautiful. But tell me truly, sister, without blandishment, am I deceiving myself when I think that I am so framed as to deserve the glory of a conquest?

AGL. You, my sister? You possess, without disguise, everything that can excite a loving passion. Your least actions are full of a charm which moves my soul. And I would be your lover if I were not a woman.

CID. Whence comes it, then, that she bears off the palm from us; that, at the first glance, all hearts give up the struggle, and that no tribute of sighs and vows is paid to our loveliness?

AGL. All the women, with one voice, find her attractions but small; and, sister, I have discovered the cause of the number of lovers she holds in thrall.

CID. I guess it. We may presume that some mystery is hidden under it. This secret of captivating everybody is not an ordinary effect of nature; the Thessalian art must be mixed up in it, and, doubtless, some one has given to her a charm by which she makes herself beloved.

AGL. My opinion is founded on a more solid basis, and the charms by which she draws all hearts to herself are a demeanour at all times free of reserve; caressing words and looks; a smile full of sweetness, which invites everyone, and promises them nothing but favours. Our glory is departed; and that lofty pride which, by a full observance of noble trials, exacted a proof of the constancy of our lovers, exists no longer. We have degenerated, and are now reduced to hope for nothing unless we throw ourselves into the arms of the men.

CID. Yes, that is the secret; and I see that you understand it better than I. It is because we cling too much to modesty, sister, that no lovers come to us; it is because we try to sustain too strictly the honour of our sex and of our birth. Men, nowadays, like what comes easily to them; hope attracts them more than love; and that is how

Psyche deprives us of all the lovers we see under her sway. Let us follow her example, and suit ourselves to the times; let us stoop, sister, to make advances, and let us no longer keep to those dull morals which rob us of the fruits of our best years.

AGL. I approve of this idea; and we have an opportunity of making a first trial of it upon the two princes who have last arrived. They are charming, sister, and to me their whole person.... Have you noticed them?

CID. Ah! Both are formed in such a mould that my soul.... They are perfect, my sister.

AGL. I think we might seek their affections without dishonour to ourselves.

CID. I think that, without shame, a beautiful princess might bestow her heart upon them.

AGL. Here they both are. I admire their manners and attire.

CID. They in no way fall short of all that we have said of them.

SCENE II. — —CLEOMENES, AGENOR, AGLAURA, CIDIPPE.

AGL. Wherefore, princes, wherefore do you thus hasten away? Does our appearance fill you with fear?

CLE. We were led to believe, Madam, that the Princess Psyche might be here.

AGL. Has this place no longer any charm for you if it is not adorned by her presence?

AGE. This place may be pleasant enough, but in our impatience we would find the Princess Psyche.

CID. Something very important must doubtless be urging you both to seek her.

CLE. The motive is powerful enough, since our happiness depends entirely upon her.

AGL. Might we be allowed to inquire into the secret implied by these words?

CLE. We do not pretend to make a mystery of it. Indeed, it would show itself in spite of us; and the secret, Madam, does not last long when it is love.

CID. Without further words, Princes, it means that you are both in love with Psyche.

AGE. We are both under her sway, and we go with one accord to declare our passion to her.

AGL. It is certainly something quite new, and rather odd, to see two rivals so well agreed.

CLE. It is true that the thing is rare; but it is not impossible for two perfect friends.

CID. In this spot, is she the only fair one, and can you find none other with whom to divide your admiration?

AGL. Amongst all the nobly born, is she the only one whom your eyes deem worthy of your tenderness?

CLE. Do we reason when we fall in love? Do we choose the object of our attachment? And when we bestow our hearts, do we weigh the right of the fair one to fascinate us?

AGE. Without having the power of choosing, we follow in such a passion something which delights us; and when love touches a heart, we have no reasons to give.

AGL. Indeed, I pity the painful troubles to which I see your hearts expose themselves. You love one whose bright charms will mingle grief with the hopes they hold out to you, and whose heart will not fulfil all that her eyes promise.

CID. The hope which calls you into the rank of her lovers will experience many disappointments in the favours she bestows; and the fitful changes of her inconstant heart will cause you many painful hours.

AGL. A clear discernment of your worth makes us pity the fate into which this passion will lead you; and if you wished, you could both find a more constant heart and charms as great.

CID. A choice sweeter by half can rescue your mutual friendship from love; and there is such a rare merit apparent in you both that a gentle counsel would, out of pity, save your hearts from what they are preparing for themselves.

CLE. This generous advice shows us a kindness which touches our hearts; but heaven, madam, reduces us to the misfortune of not being able to profit by it.

AGE. Your illustrious pity would in vain dissuade us from a love of which we both dread the result. What our friendship, Madam, has not done cannot be effected by any other means.

CID. The power of Psyche must have … Here she is.

SCENE III.— —PSYCHE, CIDIPPE, AGLAURA, CLE-OMENES, AGENOR.

CID. Come, sister, and enjoy what is offered to you.

AGL. Prepare your charms to receive here a new triumph.

CID. These two princes have both so well felt the power of your beauty that their lips are eager to declare it.

PSY. I little thought myself to be the cause of their pensiveness, and I should have expected it to be quite otherwise when I found them talking to you.

AGL. We have neither sufficient rank nor beauty to make us deserving of their love and solicitude, but they favour us with the honour of their confidence.

CLE. (*to* PSYCHE). The avowal which we would make to your divine charms, Madam, is, no doubt, a rash one; but so many hearts, on the point of expiring, are by such avowals obliged to displease you, that you have ceased to punish them by the terrors of your wrath. You see in us two friends who were joined in childhood by a happy similarity of feeling, and this tender union has been strengthened by a hundred contests of esteem and gratitude. The attachment of our friendship has been proved in the severe assaults of unfavourable fortune, the contempt of death, the sight of torture, and the glorious splendour of mutual good offices; but whatever trials it may have endured, to-day witnesses its greatest triumph, and nothing proves so much its tried fidelity as its duration through the rivalry of love. Yes, in spite of so many charms, its constancy subjects our vows to the laws it gives us. It comes with sweet and entire deference, to submit the success of our passion to your choice; and, to give a weight to our competition which may bring the balance of state reasons to favour the choice of one of us, this friendship intends of free will to unite our two estates to the fortune of the happy one.

AGE. Yes, Madam, we wish to make of these two estates, which we propose to unite under your happy choice, a help towards obtaining you. The sacrifice which we make to the king, your father, in order to ensure this happiness, has nothing difficult in it to our loving hearts, and it will be a necessary gift that the rejected unfortunate should make over to the one who is fortunate a power which he will no longer know bow to enjoy.

PSY. Princes, you both display to my eyes a choice so precious and dazzling that it would satisfy the proudest heart. But your passion, your friendship, your supreme virtue, all increase the value of your vows of fidelity, and make it a merit that I should oppose myself to what you ask of me. I must not listen to my heart only before engaging in such a union, but my hand must await my father's decision before it can dispose of itself, and my sisters have rights superior to mine. But if I were referred absolutely to my own wishes, you might both have too great a share in them, and my entire esteem be so evenly balanced between you that I should not be able to decide in favour of either. I would indeed respond with most affectionate interest to the ardour of your suit, but amid so much merit two hearts are too much for me, one heart too little for you. The accomplishment of my dearest wishes would be to me a burden were it granted to me by your love. Yes, Princes, I should greatly prefer you to all those whose love will follow yours, but I could never have the heart to prefer one of you to the other. My tenderness would be too great a sacrifice to the one whom I might choose, and I should think myself barbarously unjust to inflict so great a wrong upon the other. Indeed, you both possess such greatness of soul that it would be wrong to make either of you miserable, and you must seek in love the means of being both happy. If your hearts honour me enough to give me the right of disposing of them, I have two sisters well fitted to please, who might make your destinies happy, and whom friendship endears to me enough for me to wish that you should be their husbands.

CLE. Can a heart whose love, alas! is extreme, consent to be given away by her it loves? We yield up our two hearts, Madam, to your divine charms, even should you doom them to death; but we beg you not to make them over to any one but yourself.

AGE. It would be too unjust to the princesses, Madam, and too poor a tribute to their charms, if we should give to them the remains of a former affection. Only the faithful purity of a first love deserves to aspire to the honour to which your kindness invites us, for each of your sisters merits a love which has sighed for her alone.

AGL. It seems to me, Princes, without any offence, that before thus refusing, you might wait until our intentions had been declared. Do you think our hearts so susceptible and tender? And when people propose your offering yourselves to us, are you so sure of being accepted?

CID. I think our sentiments are lofty enough to lead us to refuse a heart which wants soliciting; and we wish to conquer our lovers by the power of our own merit.

SCENE IV.——PSYCHE, AGLAURA, CIDIPPE, CLE-OMENES, AGENOR, LYCAS.

LYC. (*to* PSYCHE). Ah! Madam!

PSY. What is the matter?

LYC. The king …

PSY. What?

LYC. Requests your presence.

PSY. What am I to augur from your agitation?

LYC. You will know it only too soon.

PSY. Alas! how you excite my fears about the king!

LYC. Fear only for yourself; you are the one to be pitied.

PSY. I can praise heaven, and be no longer anxious, when I know that I am the only one in danger. But tell me, Lycas, what alarms you.

LYC. Suffer me, Madam, to obey him who sent me hither; and I beg of you, learn from his lips what troubles me thus.

PSY. Let us go and hear what this is which makes them fear that my courage will fail me.

SCENE V. — — AGLAURA, CIDIPPE, LYCAS.

AGL. If your orders do not extend to us, tell us what great misfortune is hidden under your sadness.

LYC. Alas! hear for yourselves, princesses, the great misfortune which is known to the whole court. These are the very words which, through the oracle, destiny has spoken to the king, and which grief, Madam, has engraven on my heart: —

"No one must think to lead
Psyche to Hymen's shrine;
But all with earnest speed,
In pompous mournful line,
High to the mountain crest
Must take her; there to await,
Forlorn, in deep unrest,
A monster who envenoms all,
Decreed by fate her husband;
A serpent whose dark poisonous breath
And rage e'er hold the world in thrall,
Shaking the heavens high and realms of death."

After so severe a decree, I leave you to judge for yourselves if the gods could have manifested their wrath in a more cruel and fearful manner.

SCENE VII.— —AGLAURA, CIDIPPE.

Cid. How does this sudden misfortune into which destiny has plunged Psyche affect you, sister?

Agl. But how does it affect you, sister?

Cid. To speak the truth, my heart is not very much grieved at it.

Agl. My heart feels something which very much resembles joy. Let us go; Fate has sent us a calamity which we can consider as a blessing.

FIRST INTERLUDE.

The scenery changes to horrible rocks, and shows a dreadful cavern in the distance. It is in this desert that Psyche, *in obedience to the oracle, is to be exposed. A band of afflicted people come to bewail her death. Some give utterance to their pity by touching complaints and mournful lays, while the rest express their grief by a dance full of every mark of the most violent despair.*

WAILINGS *sung by a woman and two men.*

Woman.
Ah! weep with me, ye forests;
Ye mighty rocks of hardest adamant,
Ye Springs, ye beasts,
Lament the fate of one so fair.

1st Man.
Alas! dire grief

2nd Man.
Without relief!

1st Man.
Cruel death!

2nd Man.
Fell decree

ALL THREE (*together*).
Of sternest fate that dooms to die
Such beauty rare! Oh! heavens high!
And stars! behold! and sigh!

WOMAN.
My sad, sad lay repeat,
  Ye caverns deep;
With notes of sorrow greet
  Her death, ye mountains steep;
Re-echo, woods, and silent hills,
My grief; and ye, soft rippling rills!

1ST MAN.
Alas! dire grief

2ND MAN.
Without relief!

1ST MAN.
Cruel death!

2ND MAN.
Fell decree

ALL THREE (*together*).
Of sternest fate that dooms to die
Such beauty rare! Oh! heavens high!
And stars! behold! and sigh!

2ND MAN.
Who then, eternal gods, will doom
A guiltless maid to lasting gloom?
Oh! this thy rigour, heaven, shames
Hell's unrelenting flames!

1ST MAN.
Cruel will

2ND MAN.
Of gods severe!

THE TWO MEN.
Say why this hard decree,

To crush a heart so free
    From guilt or stain?
Oh! fell edict unheard ere this!
Thou doomest a maid who showers bliss
  Upon the mortal race.
  She the sad earth would grace,
    And would give life for pain!

WOMAN.
All tears are idle, all sighs.
Heaven wills it so—she dies!
Whene'er the gods their powers wield,
All man can do—is but to yield.

1ST MAN.
Alas! dire grief

2ND MAN.
Without relief!

1ST MAN.
Cruel death!

2ND MAN.
Fell decree!

ACT II.

SCENE I.——THE KING, PSYCHE, AGLAURA, CIDIPPE, LYCAS, *and* FOLLOWERS.

PSY. The cause of your tears, my Lord, is dear to me; but you are too kind when you allow a father's love to overmaster the duties of a great king. The homage which here you pay to nature is fraught with too much injury to the rank which you hold. I must decline its touching favours. Check somewhat the sway of your grief over your wisdom, and cease to honour my destiny with tears, which, springing from a king's heart, show weakness.

KING. Ah! my daughter! close not my eyes to these tears; my grief is reasonable, even though it be extreme; and when such a loss as mine must endure for ever, wisdom herself, believe me, may weep. 'Tis in vain that pride of regal sway bids us be insensible to such calamities; as vain for reason to come to our help, and desire us to see with unmoved eye the death of what we love. The effort required is barbarous in the eyes of the universe — 'tis brutality rather than highest virtue. In this misfortune I will not wear a show of insensibility, and hide the grief I feel. I renounce the vanity of this fierce callousness, known as fortitude, and whatever be the name given to the keen pain, the pangs of which I feel, I will exhibit it, my daughter, to the gaze of all, and in the heart of a king display that of a man.

PSY. I deserve not this violent grief. Seek, I pray, to resist the claims it asserts over your heart, whose might a thousand events have marked. What! for me, my Lord, you must abandon that kingly firmness of which, under the blows of misfortune, you have shown such perfect proofs?

KING. In numberless occasions firmness is easy. All revolutions to which ruthless fortune can expose us — loss of rank, persecution, envy's venom, hatred's dart — present nothing which the will of a soul, but a little swayed by reason, cannot easily brave. But those rigours which crush the heart under the weight of bitter grief are ... are the cruel darts of those severe decrees of fate which deprive us for ever of our loved ones. Against such ills reason offers no available weapons. These are the direst blows that the gods in their wrath can hurl against us!

PSY. My Lord, one consolation is still left you. Your marriage has been graced with more than one gift from the gods, and by hiding me from your sight, they with open favour deprive you of nothing but what they have not carefully made good for you. Enough remains to relieve your sorrow, and this law of heaven which you call cruel leaves sufficient room in the two princesses, my sisters, for paternal love wherein to place all its kindness.

KING. Ah! empty comfort to my sorrow. There is naught that can console me for thy loss. My grief fills my soul, I am conscious of nothing else; in presence of such cruel destiny, I look to what I lose, and see not what I still retain.

PSY. My Lord, you know better than myself that we must rule our will by that of heaven; and in this sad farewell I can only say to you that which you can much better say to others. These gods are sovereign lords of the gifts they deign to offer us; they leave them in our hands so long only as it pleases them; when they withdraw them, we have no right to murmur over the favours which their hands refuse any longer to pour upon us. My Lord, I am a gift they have offered to your vows, and when, by this decree, they wish to take me back, they deprive you of nothing that you do not hold from them; and it is without a murmur that you must resign me.

KING. Ah! seek, I pray, better foundations for the comfort thy heart would offer me. Do not by the fallacy of thy reasoning increase the burden of the piercing grief which now torments me. Dost thou imagine that thou givest me a powerful reason why I should not complain of this decree of heaven? and in this proceeding of the gods, of which thou biddest me be satisfied, dost thou not clearly see a deadly severity? Consider the state in which the gods force me to resign thee, and that in which my hapless heart received thee. Thou shalt know then that they take from me much more than they gave: from them I received in thee, my daughter, a gift I did not ask for; then I found in it but few charms, and without joy I saw my family increased by it. But my heart and my eyes have made a sweet habit of this gift. Fifteen years of care, of watchfulness, of study, have I employed to render it precious to me. I have decked it with the lovely wealth of a thousand brilliant virtues; I have enshrined in it, by assiduous care, the rarest treasures that wisdom yields; to it clings the tenderness of my soul. I have made it the charm, the joy of this heart, the solace of my wearied senses, the sweet hope of my old age. All this they take from me—these gods! And thou wouldst have me utter no complaint concerning this dire edict from which I suffer! Ah! with too much rigour their power tramples upon the affections of our heart. To withdraw their gift, have they not waited till I had made it my all? Rather, if it was their purpose to remove it, had it not been better to give me nothing?

Psy. My Lord! dread the wrath of those gods whom you dare upbraid.

King. After this blow, what more can they inflict on me?

Psy. Ah! my Lord! I tremble for your sins, of which I am the cause; I hate myself for this....

King. Ah! let them bear with my legitimate complaints; 'tis pain enough for me to obey them; it ought to suffice them that my heart abandons thee to the barbarous respect we must bear them, without claiming also to control the grief that so frightful a decree calls forth. My just despair can know no bounds. My grief, my grief, I will nurse it for ever! I will feel for ever the loss I sustain, of heaven's rigour I will always raise high my complaint; until death I will unceasingly weep for that than which the whole world could give me naught more precious.

Psy. +Ah! I pray you, my Lord, spare my weakness. I need constancy in these circumstances. Add not to the excess of my grief by the tears of your fondness. My sorrow alone is deep enough; my fate and your grief are too much for my heart.

King. True! I must spare thee my disconsolate trouble. The fatal moment has come. I must tear myself from thee; but how can I utter this dreadful word? And yet I must! Heaven commands it. An unavoidable cruelty forces me to leave thee in this fatal spot. Farewell, I go.... Farewell.

SCENE II. — — PSYCHE, AGLAURA, CIDIPPE.

Psy. Follow the king, my sisters; dry his tears, solace his grief. You would fill him with alarm were you to, expose yourselves to my misfortune. Preserve for him whatever he possesses still; the serpent I expect might prove hurtful to you, and draw you in the same fate as myself; nay, through *your* death might cause me a second death. Me alone has heaven condemned to his poisonous breath; nothing could save me; and I need no example to die.

AGL. Grudge us not this cruel privilege of mingling our tears with your sorrows; suffer our sighs to answer your last sighs; accept this last pledge of our tender love.

PSY. 'Tis but to lose yourselves to no purpose.

CID. 'Tis to hope for a miracle in your favour, or to accompany you to the tomb.

PSY. What room is there for hope after such an oracle?

AGL. An oracle is ever veiled in obscurity; the more we believe that we know its meaning, the less do we understand it. Perhaps, after all, you must expect from it nothing but glory and happiness. Suffer us, dear sister, to behold this mortal dread deceived by a worthy issue; or at least let us die with you, if heaven does not show itself more propitious to our prayers.

PSY. Dear sister, lend a readier ear to nature's voice, which summons you to stand by the king. You love me too much, and duty murmurs; you know its unavoidable laws. A father ought to be dearer to you than myself; become both the mainstays of his old age. A thousand kings, a thousand rival kings, cherish love for you; you both owe your father a son-in-law and grandchildren. A thousand kings vie with each other to whisper their vows to you. Me alone the oracle demands, and alone, too, I will die, if I can, without weakness, or, if not, at least without you as witnesses of that little which nature has left me.

AGL. Then by sharing your woe we annoy you!

CID. I dare go somewhat further, we offend you!

PSY. No; but you add to my torture, and perhaps increase the wrath of heaven.

AGL. It is your will; we go. May that same heaven, more just, and less severe, decree for you the fate we desire, and for which our sincere friendship, in spite of you and of the oracle, still hopes!

PSY. Farewell. This hope, these vows, my sisters, none of the gods will ever fulfil.

SCENE III.— —PSYCHE (*alone*).

Alone, at last, I can look on this terrible change, which from the summit of highest glory hurls me to the tomb. This glory was without parallel. Its sheen spread from pole to pole; all kings seemed created to love me; all their subjects, looking upon me as on a goddess, were but now beginning to accustom me to the incense they never ceased to offer; sighs followed me, for which I gave naught in return. My soul remained fancy-free, while it captivated so many, and in the midst of so much love was queen of all hearts, and yet mistress of my own. Oh! heaven! hast thou counted a crime this want of feeling? All this severity which thou dost exhibit, is it because in return for their vows I have given nothing but esteem? If such be thy law, why didst thou not create in me that which merit and love create in others, and…. But what do I see here?

SCENE IV.— —CLEOMENES, AGENOR, PSYCHE.

CLE. Behold in us two friends, two rivals, whose only wish is to expose our life to save yours.

PSY. Can I listen to you when I have refused two sisters? Princes! think you that you could defend me against heaven? To surrender yourselves to the serpent, whose coming I must await here, is but a despair ill-becoming great hearts; and to die when I die is to overwhelm a sensitive, soul, that already has but too many sorrows.

AGE. A serpent is not invincible; Cadmus, who loved no one, slew Mars' own reptile. We love, and Love makes everything possible for the heart that follows his standard, for the hand of whose darts he is himself the guide.

PSY. Do you expect his aid in behalf of an ungrateful one whom all his shafts have been unable to wound? Think you he can stay his vengeance, when 'tis bursting forth, and help you to release me from its stroke? Even if you should serve me, even if you should restore me to life, what reward do you hope for from that which knows no love?

CLE. It is not by the hope of so lovely a reward that we are animated. We seek only to obey the dictates of a love that dares not presume, whatever its efforts may be, that it can be so fortunate as to please you, so worthy as to kindle within you a responsive flame.

Age. Live, fair princess, and live for another; we will behold it with a jealous eye, we will die of it, yet of a death sweeter far than if we had to see you die. If we cannot save your life by the loss of ours, whatever love you may prefer to ours, we are ready to die of grief and of love.

Psy. Live, Princes, live, and no longer seek to ward off or to share my fate. I believe I have told you, heaven seeks me alone; me alone has it condemned. Methinks, I hear already the deadly hissing of its minister, who even now draws nigh. My dread pictures him to me, ever offers him to my view. Fear has mastered all my feelings; under its influence I see him on the summit of this rock; I sink for very weakness, and my fainting heart scarce keeps up a remnant of courage. Farewell, Princes; flee, lest he poison you.

Age. We have seen nothing as yet to astonish us. And since you deem your death so nigh, if strength fail you, we have both arms and hearts which hope never forsakes. It may be a rival has dictated this oracle; and gold has made its interpreter speak. It would be no miracle if a man has answered in the stead of a dumb deity; and everywhere we have but too many examples that temples, no less than other places, are the abode of the wicked.

Cle. Suffer us to oppose to the cowardly ravisher to whom sacrilege abandons you a love that heaven has chosen for the defender of the only fair one for whom we wish to live. If we dare not aspire to her possession, at least, in the midst of her danger, allow us to follow the ardour and dictates of our passion.

Psy. These dictates, this extreme ardour, with which your hearts are filled in my behalf, obey them in behalf of others, in behalf of my sisters. Live for them, since I die. Lament the cruel rigour of my fate; and by your death do not give my sisters new ground for sorrow. These are my last wishes, and in all ages the orders of the dying have been received as law.

Cle. Princess....

Psy. Once more, Princes, live for my sisters. So long as you love me, you must obey me; do not drive me to hate you, and to look upon you as rebels for being too faithful to me. Go, leave me to die alone in this spot, where I have no voice left except to say farewell. But I feel myself lifted up, and the air opens a road whence you will no longer hear this dying voice. Farewell, Princes, farewell, for the last time. See, can you doubt my destiny?

PSYCHE *is borne through the air by two* ZEPHYRS.

AGE. We lose sight of her. Prince, let us both seek on the summit of this rock some means of following her.

CLE. Let us seek those of not surviving her.

SCENE V. — —LOVE (*in the air*).

LOVE. Die, then, rivals of a jealous god, whose wrath you have deserved, since your heart was sensible to the same charms. And thou, Vulcan, fashion a thousand brilliant ornaments to adorn the palace where Love will dry Psyche's tears, and yield himself her slave.

SECOND INTERLUDE.

The scene changes to a splendid terrace, surrounded by pillars emblazoned with golden figures. The whole represents a magnificent palace, which LOVE *designs for* PSYCHE. *Six* CYCLOPS, *accompanied by four* FAIRIES, *introduce a ballet, and, whilst keeping time, give the last touches to four huge silver vases which the* FAIRIES *have brought. The ballet is twice interrupted by this recitation of* VULCAN, *which he gives out in two parts*

PART I.

Hasten, these seats prepare
For heaven's gentlest god.
No strength, no effort spare;
With mighty zeal and constant care
Do now, my lads, what must be done.

When Love commands us—see!
What haste too great can be?

Great Love no lazy hand will brook;
So work with might and main.
Your ancient hammers ply,
And sparks will swiftly fly
Beneath your arms that rain
The fast, resounding blows;
While zeal to please him glows
Within your heaving breasts.

Part II.

Then serve a god so kind,
Who loves great zeal to find.
No strength, no effort spare;
With mighty zeal and constant care
Do now, my lads, what must be done.
When Love commands us—see!
What haste too great can be?

Great Love no lazy hand can brook;
So work with might and main.
Your ancient hammers ply,
And sparks will swiftly fly
Beneath your arms that rain
The fast, resounding blows,
While zeal to please him glows;
Within your heaving breasts.

ACT III.

SCENE I.——LOVE, ZEPHYR.

Zep. Yes! right gallantly have I acquitted myself of your errand;
and from the summit of that rock I have softly borne this beauty

through the air to this enchanted palace, where, with full freedom, you can decree her fate. Yet you astonish me by this mighty change in your appearance. That figure, that countenance, that costume, perfectly conceal your real being, and I defy the most cunning to see in you to-day the god of love.

LOVE. 'Tis because I do not wish to be known to Psyche. 'Tis my heart, my heart alone, I wish to unfold; nothing more than the sweet raptures of this keen passion, which her charms excite within it. To express its gentle pining, and to hide what may be from those eyes that impose on me their will, I have assumed this form which thou seest.

ZEP. You are a master in everything; this is how I know it. Often the gods, when in love, have been seen assuming various disguises, seeking to alleviate the pleasing wound inflicted on all hearts by your fiery darts; but in good sense you outstrip them. Yours is the form necessary for succeeding with the lovely sex, for whom we sigh. Yes, the assistance derived from that form is powerful; and, apart from rank and wit, whoever finds the means of being so fashioned does not sigh in vain.

LOVE. I have decided, my dear Zephyr, to remain always thus; and the oldest of all loves cannot be blamed for this. It is time to issue from this long infancy, that wears out my patience. It is time, henceforth, that I should be grown up.

ZEP. You are right. You cannot do better; and you are initiated into a mystery that demands no childish powers.

LOVE. This change will, no doubt, vex my mother.

ZEP. I foresee some anger in that quarter, although disputes about age ought not to exist among immortals; yet, your mother Venus shares the spirit of beauties, who do not like grown-up children. But whereat I fancy her offended is the line of conduct you are pursuing; and 'tis a strange method of avenging her, to love the beauty she wished to see punished. This hatred to which she expects the power of a son generally feared by the gods to answer….

LOVE. Let us drop this discourse, Zephyr, and tell me whether thy eyes do not find Psyche the fairest woman in the world? Is there aught on the earth, aught in heaven, that could seize from her the glorious title of matchless beauty? But I see her, my dear Zephyr, wondering at the splendours of this spot.

Zep. You can show yourself, to put an end to her torture, and unfold to her her glorious destiny. Speak to one another all that sighs, lips, and glances can speak. As a discreet confident, I know my duty, and will not interrupt lovers' secrets.

SCENE II.— —PSYCHE (*alone*).

Where am I? and in a spot I deemed deserted, what skilled hand has reared this palace, which art and nature deck with the rarest gifts that the eye could ever admire. Everything smiles, shines, sparkles in this garden, in these apartments, whose pompous furniture presents nothing that does not charm and flatter the beholder; and whithersoever my fears lead me, I see under my feet naught but gold or flowers. Can heaven have formed this world of wonders for the abode of a serpent? And when, by this sight, it amuses and stays the unequalled rigour of my jealous fate, does it wish to show that it repents of it? No, no; this is the darkest, the keenest shaft of its hatred, so fertile in its cruelties. This hatred, by a renewed and unparalleled sternness, lays before my gaze the choice it has made of all that is fairest in the world, only that I may leave it with deeper regret.

How foolish is my hope if it fancies it can thus alleviate my pain. Every moment that my death is delayed becomes a new misfortune for me; the more it stays its coming, the oftener I die.

Leave me no longer to pine; come, take thy victim, monster, whose mission it is to slay me. Wouldst thou have me seek thee? and must I rouse thy fury to devour me? If heaven wills my death, if my life be a crime, dare at length to seize whatever little remains of it; I am tired of murmuring against a lawful penalty; I am weary of sighs; come, that I may end the death I am dying.

SCENE III. — —LOVE, PSYCHE, ZEPHYR.

Love. Behold this serpent, this pitiless monster, whom a wonderful oracle has prepared for you, and who perhaps does not inspire such dread as you had imagined.

Psy. You, my Lord! you are that monster who, so spoke the oracle, threatens my sad life? you, who seem rather a god, deigning miraculously to come yourself to my rescue?

Love. What need of help in the midst of an empire where all that breathes only awaits your look to do its bidding, where I am the only monster you have to fear?

Psy. But small is the fear that a monster like you inspires, and if it has any venom, a soul has little reason to venture on the least complaint against a pleasing poison, the cure of which all the heart would dread! Scarce do I behold you than already my calmed fears suffer the image of death to vanish; and I feel I know not what unknown fire flow through my frozen veins: Esteem I have felt, and kindness, friendship, gratitude; compassion's innocent sorrows have made me know its power, but I have not yet felt what I now feel. I know not what it is, but I know that it fills me with delight, and causes me no alarm. The longer I gaze on you, the more I feel the spell. Nothing that I have ever felt had the same effect; and I would tell you, my Lord, that I love you, did I know what love is. Turn them not away, those eyes that poison me, those eyes so tender, so piercing, yet so loving, that look as if they shared the confusion they cause me. Alas! the more dangerous they prove, the more fondly I cling to them. What decree of heaven is it which I cannot understand, that forces me to tell you more than I should? I, whose modesty ought at least to wait that you explain the confusion that, I see, is within you. You sigh, my Lord, as I sigh; your senses, like mine, seem amazed. 'Tis my duty to be silent concerning this, yours to speak it, yet it is I who tell this to you.

Love. Your heart, Psyche, has ever been too insensible, and you must not wonder if, to repair the insult, Love now pays himself with usury for that which your soul ought to have granted him. The time is come in which your lips must breathe those sighs so long restrained; and while it draws you from that fierce humour, an endless rapture, as sweet as it is unknown, must wound you as deeply as it ought to have wounded you during those golden days the course of which your unfeeling soul has profaned.

PSY. Not to love is, then, a great crime?

LOVE. Do you suffer a hard punishment for it?

PSY. The punishment is mild indeed.

LOVE. The penalty is suited to the offence; and Love, on this glorious day, avenges himself of lack of love by an excess of love.

PSY. Would I had been punished before! My life's happiness lies in it. I ought to blush at it, or to whisper it low, but this torture has too many charms. Suffer me to say, and to repeat it aloud; though I said it a hundred times, I would never blush for it. It is not I who speak; and the wonderful empire, the amiable violence of your presence, sway my voice as soon as I begin to speak. Vainly does my modesty take secret offence at it; vainly would my sex and decency bind me to other laws; it is your eyes that dictate my answer, and my lips, the slaves of their almighty power, no longer consult me on the self-respect I owe myself.

LOVE. Fair Psyche, believe what these eyes tell you. Let yours vie with each other in instructing me of all your emotions. Trust this sighing heart, which, so long as yours will answer, will tell you more by a sigh than a hundred looks can express. 'Tis the sweetest language, the most powerful, the truest of all!

PSY. The understanding of it was due to both our hearts to make them equally satisfied. I have sighed, you have understood me; you sigh, and I heard you. But release me from doubt, my Lord, and tell me, if by the same road Zephyr has led you hither after me; to tell me what I hear now. When I arrived here, were you expected? and when you speak to him, are you obeyed?

LOVE. The empire I exercise over this sweet climate is as sovereign as yours is over my heart. *Love* is favourable to me, and 'tis for his sake that Aeolus has placed Zephyr under my command. It was Love who, to reward my passion, dictated this oracle, by which your fair days that were threatened have been released from a throng of lovers; and which has freed me from the lasting obstacle of so many ardent sighs that were unworthy of being addressed to you. Ask not of me what this region be, nor the name of its ruler; you shall know it in time. My object is to win you; but I wish to do so by my services, my assiduous care, my constant vows, by a lover's sacrifice of all that I am, of all my power can effect. The splendour of my rank must not solicit you for me, neither must I make a merit of my power; and though sovereign lord of this blissful realm, I wish to owe you, Psyche, to nothing but my love.

Come with me, Princess, and admire its marvels; prepare your eyes and ears to the charms it will offer you. You shall gaze on woods and meads, contesting their beauties with gold and gems; you shall hear nothing but sweet concerts; a hundred beauties shall serve you here; without envy they shall worship you, and every moment with a humble and raptured soul shall solicit the honour of your commands.

Psy. My will waits upon yours; I can no longer have one of my own; but at any rate your oracle has severed me from two sisters, and the king, my father, whom my supposed death has all three reduced to bewail me. Suffer my sisters to be witnesses of my glory and your love for me, to dissipate the error which overwhelms their soul with mortal sorrow.

Lend them too, as you did me, Zephyr's wings, that they may facilitate their access to your empire, as they did mine. Let them see where I live, let them wonder at the success of my loss.

Love. You do not yield me all your soul, Psyche. This affectionate remembrance of a father and two sisters snatches from me part of that which I crave for my passion only. Have no eyes for anyone but for me, who have none but for you. Let love for me, and the desire of pleasing me, be your only thought, and when such cares dare divert you from it….

Psy. Can you be jealous of affection for kin?

Love. I am jealous, my Psyche, jealous of all nature. The sun's rays kiss you too often; your tresses are too sensible to the wooing of the breeze; no sooner does it caress them than I murmur. The very air which you breathe passes with too much pleasure between your lips; your robes cling too closely to your form. I know not what bewilders me, and I dread amidst your sighs some stray one.

But you would see your sisters. Be gone, Zephyr; Psyche commands, I cannot forbid.

SCENE IV. — — LOVE, PSYCHE.

LOVE. When you shall show them this blissful seat, make them a thousand gifts from these treasures; lavish on them endearments, caresses; and, if possible, exhaust the tendernesses that blood demands, so that you may yield yourself entirely to love. I shall not importune you with my presence, but let not your meeting be too long, remembering that you rob *me* of whatever attention you pay *them*.

PSY. Your love grants me a favour, which 'twere not possible for me to abuse.

LOVE. Still, let us visit these gardens, this palace, where you will meet naught but what will pale before your dazzling charms. And you, little Cupids, you, young Zephyrs, whose souls are but soft sighs, vie with each other in showing what joy you feel at the appearance of my princess.

THIRD INTERLUDE.

Entry of ballet, composed of four CUPIDS *and four* ZEPHYRS, *twice interrupted by a dialogue sung by a* CUPID *and a* ZEPHYR.

LOVE, PSYCHE.

PART I.

A ZEPHYR.

Ye gentle youth, follow
Love's sweet and tender glow;
In happy days and fair,
From passion's joys do not forbear. —
'Tis to deceive they tell you, aye,
You should avoid the wooing sigh,
And fear the pressing suit. —

'Tis now the time to learn
What fires within you burn!

They sing together.

All gentle hearts in turn
With love must glow;
And greater charms that burn
A greater debt will owe.

A ZEPHYR (alone).

A youthful heart and tender
At last must yield surrender.

BOTH (together).

All gentle hearts in turn
With love must glow;
And greater charms that burn
A greater debt will owe.

A CUPID (alone).

What boots to play the truant's part,
And shield yourselves against the dart?
The sunny day is flown and gone,
The hour lost may ne'er be won.

BOTH (together).

All gentle hearts in turn
With love must glow;
And greater charms that burn
A greater debt will owe.

PART II.

A ZEPHYR (alone).

Great Love hath potent charms;
To him we yield our arms;
His cares and sorrows sweet
Have, too, their joy — though fleet!

To follow him, all hearts
Would court a thousand darts.
If we would taste his deep delight,
Ah! we must pine till fades the light
Before our eyes.
A worthless life it is—when love
Fills not the heart it fain would move!

They sing together.

In love if we must grieve and sigh,
A moment's bliss still well repays
The ills and woes of many days.

A Zephyr (alone).

'Midst hopes and fears,
And mystery and tears,
We cannot, without the touch of pain,
Bliss seek again.

Both (together).

In love if we must grieve and sigh,
A moment's bliss still well repays
The ills and woes of many days.

A Cupid (alone).

What better deed is there to do
Than strive to please and softly woo?
A lover's part is sweetest care,
And this it is that all must bear.

Both (together).

In love if we must grieve and sigh,
A moment's bliss still well repays
The ills and woes of many days.

ACT IV.

The scene changes to a splendid palace, in the interior of which is seen at the end of a long vestibule a lovely garden, in which are many trees laden with all kinds of fruit.

SCENE I. — — AGLAURA, CIDIPPE.

AGL. I can bear it no longer, my sister. I have seen too many wonders; future times will scarcely conceive them; this sun, that sees all, and lays all before our gaze, never beheld the like. This dazzling palace and this stately equipage are a display hateful to me; shame as well as spite overwhelm me. How cruelly Fortune has treated us; see how her inconsiderate bounty blindly lavishes, exhausts, and unites her efforts to make all these treasures the lot of a younger sister!

CID. I share all your feelings; your griefs are mine; in this delightful spot, all that displeases you wounds me; all which you consider a deadly insult oppresses me no less than yourself, and leaves bitterness within my breast and blushes on my brow.

AGL. No, my sister, no living queen, in her own realm speaks in such sovereign tones as Psyche in these abodes. Here we see her obeyed with scrupulous exactitude; and a yearning study of her will seeks it even in her eyes, a thousand beauties throng around her, and seem to say to our jealous looks, "Whatever your charms may be, she is still fairer, and we who serve her are fairer than you." She orders, it is done; none refuse, none rebel. Flora, clinging to her steps, lavishes her sweetest charms around her; Zephyr flies to execute her orders, and his mistress and he, too much a prey to her charms, forget their own love in their eagerness to serve her.

CID. She has gods at her services, soon she will have altars; our sway extends over weak mortals only, whose continual caprice and impudence, rebelling secretly from us, oppose either murmurs or stratagem to our will.

AGL. It was but little indeed that at our court so many hearts contended for her, preferring her to us! It was not enough that she was there worshipped night and day by a crowd of lovers. When we were comforting ourselves with seeing her on the brink of the grave by the sudden order of the oracle, she thought fit to display before us the miracle of her new destiny, and has chosen our eyes to be witnesses of that which at the bottom of our hearts we least desire.

CID. What above all fills my heart with despair is to see this lover, so perfect, so born to please, a captive under her sway. Were it in our power to choose from so many monarchs, should we find one who bears such a noble mien? To see your wishes fulfilled beyond expectation is oftentimes a bliss that engenders unhappiness; there is no splendid train, no proud palace, but opens some door to incurable ills. But to possess a lover of perfect merit, to see yourself dearly beloved by him, is a happiness so lofty, so exquisite, that its worth cannot be expressed.

AGL. No more of this, my sister; the thought of it would kill us; let us rather think of revenge; let us find means of breaking the spell that fosters this affection between her and him.

She comes; I have darts ready, such as she shall find difficult to parry.

SCENE II.— —PSYCHE, AGLAURA, CIDIPPE.

PSY. I come to bid you farewell; my lover wishes your departure. He can no longer endure that you should deprive him of a particle of the joy he feels in being alone to contemplate me. The merest look, the slightest word, is a treasure for his love, and I rob him of it when I grant it to my sisters in favour of the ties of blood.

AGL. Jealousy is very keen, and these nice sentiments well deserve that he who shows such tenderness for you should be considered above the generality of lovers. I speak thus because I do not know him; nor do you know his name, or that of those to whom he owes the light. This alarms us. I hold him to be a mighty prince, whose power is extreme, far above kingly sway. His treasure which he has strewn beneath your feet would put Abundance herself to the blush. Your love for him is as keen as his for you; you are his delight, he is yours; your happiness, my sister, would be perfect if you but knew whom you love.

Psy. What care I! He loves me. The more he sees me, the more I please him. There are no pleasures which delight the soul, but anticipate my wishes. I do not understand the cause of your alarm when all here obeys my will.

Agl. What boots it that all bows to you here if this lover ever conceals what he is? If we are alarmed, it is for your interest alone. Vain it is that everything meets you with a smile, and brings delight; true love scorns reserve; and whoever persists in concealment is conscious that he is in some way open to reproach. Should this suitor prove fickle—for often change in love is pleasing, and between ourselves, I dare say that, however dazzling the flash of your charms, there are others as fair as you—if, I say, another beauty should bind him under new thralls, if in the state in which you are now, alone and defenceless at his mercy, he should go so far as to offer violence, on whom should the king wreak his vengeance for this change or this insolence?

Psy. You fill me with dread. Kind heaven! can I be so unfortunate?

Cid. Who knows but that Hymen's knot....

Psy. Say no more, I could not bear it.

Agl. I have but one word more to say. This prince who loves you, sways the winds, gives us Zephyr's wings for a chariot, and every moment lavishes on you new pleasures, when he thus openly breaks the order of nature, may perhaps mingle some little imposture with so much love. Perhaps this palace is nothing more than an enchantment; these gilt ceilings, these mountains of wealth, with which he buys your affection, so soon as he shall be weary of your caresses, will vanish in a moment. You know as well as ourselves what power lies in spells.

Psy. In my turn, what cruel alarms I feel!

Agl. Our friendship seeks your good only.

Psy. Farewell, sisters, we must close our meeting; I love, and fear lest he should grow impatient; go, and to-morrow, if I may, you shall see me, either happier or crushed by the deepest anguish.

AGL. We go to apprise the king of the new glory, the excess of bliss which heaven showers upon you.

CID. We go to relate to him the surprising and marvellous tale of so pleasing a change.

PSY. Trouble him not, sisters, with your suspicions, and when you describe to him this charming empire….

AGL. We both know what we must conceal and what speak, and need no lessons.

ZEPHYR carries off PSYCHE'S sisters in a cloud, which descends to the earth, and in which he bears them rapidly away.

SCENE III. — — LOVE, PSYCHE.

LOVE. You are alone at last. I can once more without your importunate sisters as witnesses declare to you what sway eyes so fair have won over me, and how extreme is the delight that a sincere ardour inspires when once it has locked two hearts together. I can unfold to you the loving eagerness of my enraptured soul, and swear that, enslaved to you alone, its rapture has no other aim than to behold this ardour followed by a similar ardour, to conceive no other wish but to bind my vows to your desires, and make all that pleases you my only delight. But wherefore does a cloud of sadness seem to dim the brightness of those beautiful eyes? Is there aught which you can want in these abodes? Scorn you the homage of the vows here paid to you?

PSY. No, my Lord!

LOVE. What is it then? And to what must I attribute my misfortune? You sigh less from love than from grief. The roses of your cheek are faded, a token of secret sorrow. Scarce are your sisters gone than you sigh of regret. Ah! my Psyche, when two hearts are swayed by an equal passion, can their sighs have a different object? and when their love is true, and the loved one nigh, is there room to sigh for relatives?

PSY. That is not the cause of my sorrow.

LOVE. Is it the absence of a rival, and a favoured rival too, that causes this neglect?

PSY. How ill you understand a heart wholly yours. I love you, my Lord; and my love is vexed at the undeserved suspicion which you have conceived. You but little know your own deserts, if you fear that you are not loved. I love you; and since I beheld the light of day, I have shown myself proud enough to scorn the vows of more than one king; and since I must disclose to you my whole heart, I have found none but you worthy of me. And yet I feel a certain sadness, which I would fain conceal from you; a gloomy grief is mingled with all my affection. Ask not the cause of it; perhaps, if you knew it, you would punish me for it, and if I still dare to aspire to anything, I am sure I should not obtain it.

LOVE. And do you not dread lest I should in my turn feel vexed at you for so ill understanding your own powers, or for pretending to be ignorant of the absolute sway you exercise over me? Ah! if you doubt it in the least, be undeceived. Speak.

PSY. I should have to bear with the shame of a refusal.

LOVE. I pray you to harbour kinder feelings in my behalf; the trial of it is easy. Speak; everything waits on your will. If you cannot trust my words without oaths, I swear by those beautiful eyes, those lords of my heart, those divine authors of my passion; and if it be not sufficient to swear by your beautiful eyes, I swear by the Styx, by which all the gods do swear.

PSY. After this assurance, my fears are somewhat allayed. My Lord, here I look on pomp and abundance, I adore you, and you worship me; my heart is enraptured, my senses charmed by it; but amidst this highest bliss, I have the misfortune of not knowing which it is whom I love. Dispel this darkness, and unfold to me who this perfect lover is.

LOVE. Psyche, what is that you say?

PSY. That this is the happiness for which I long, and that if you refuse it to me …

Love. I have sworn it, I am no longer master of it; but you do not know what you ask. Leave me my secret. If I discover myself, I lose you and you me. The only remedy is for you to retract your words.

Psy. Is this my sovereign sway over you?

Love. Your power is unbounded, and I am wholly yours. But if our wooing has charms for you, lay no obstacle in the way of its pleasing continuance. Do not force me to flight. This would be the least misfortune which can happen to us from that wish which has seduced you.

Psy. My Lord, you now wish to test me; but I know how far I am to believe it. I pray you to let me know the measure of my glory, and no longer to conceal from me for what illustrious choice I have rejected the vows of so many kings.

Love. Do you will it so?

Psy. Suffer me to beseech you to it.

Love. If you knew what cruel misfortune you draw upon yourself by it....

Psy. My Lord, you fill me with despair.

Love. Think well on it; I can yet be silent.

Psy. Do you pledge yourself by oaths which you do not mean to keep.

Love. Be it so! I am a god, the most powerful of all gods, absolute master on this earth, and in the heavens; my power is supreme in the ocean and the air; in a word, I am Love himself. I have wounded myself with my own darts for love of you; and, alas! but for the violence which you impose on me, and which has turned my passion for you into wrath, you would have me now for your husband. Your wish is accomplished; you know whom you loved; you know the lover whom you charmed; see now what misfortune is upon us. Yourself you force me to abandon you, yourself you force me to deprive you of all the fruits of your victory. It may be that your beautiful eyes will see me no more; this palace, these grounds, once vanished with me, will cause your rising glory to fade away. You would not believe me, and the dispelling of this doubt has for fruit that Fate, at whose blows the very heavens tremble, mightier than my love, mightier than all the gods united, which is even now showing its hatred to you, and driving me hence.

LOVE *flies away, and the gardens vanish.*

SCENE IV.

The stage represents a desert and the wild banks of a river.

PSYCHE, *the* RIVER GOD, *reclining on a bank of reeds, and leaning on an urn.*

PSY. Cruel destiny! aching pain! fatal curiosity! Speak, dread solitude, what hast thou done with all my felicity? I loved a god; was beloved by him; my happiness redoubled at every moment; and now behold me, alone, bewailing, in the midst of a desert, where, to increase my pain, when shame and despair are upon me, I feel my love increasing now that I have lost the lover. Its very remembrance charms and poisons my soul. Its delights tyrannise over a wretched heart, which my passion has condemned to the keenest pain. Kind heaven! When Love abandoned me, why did he leave me the fire he had breathed into me. O thou! the pure and inexhaustible source of all good, lord of men and gods, dear author of the pain I now endure, art thou for ever vanished from my sight? I! I banished thee! when love was deepest, when bliss supreme, an unworthy suspicion filled my heart with alarm. Ungrateful heart, the fire was but ill-kindled; for from the first moment of love we cannot have any wish other than that of him whom we cherish. Let me die, it is the only choice left me after the loss I have made. For whom, great gods, would I live, for whom entertain a single wish? Thou, river, whose wave washes these desert sands, bury my crime in thy waters; and end ills so miserable by allowing me to find a rest in thy bed.

THE RIVER GOD. Thy death would sully my stream, Psyche. Heaven forbids it. Perhaps after such heavy sorrows, another fate awaits thee. Rather flee Venus' implacable anger. I see her seeking thee in order to punish thee; the son's love has excited the mother's hatred. Flee! I will detain her.

Psy. I shall await her avenging wrath! What can it have that will not be too pleasant for me? Whoever seeks death dreads no gods or goddesses, but can defy all their darts.

SCENE V.——VENUS, PSYCHE, THE RIVER GOD.

Ven. Insolent Psyche, you dare then to await my arrival after you have deprived me on earth of my honours, after your seducing charms have received the incense which is due to mine alone? I have seen my shrines forsaken, I have seen all the world, enslaved by your charms, idolise you as the sovereign beauty, offer to you a homage until then unknown, and not stay to consider whether there was another Venus at all; notwithstanding this, I see you bold enough not to dread the punishment your crime justly deserves, and to meet my gaze as if my resentment were but little matter.

Psy. If I have been loved by a few mortals, is it a crime in me to have possessed charms by which they allowed their eyes to be captured while they were blind to you? I am but what heaven hath made me, I have only those attractions which it has been willing to lend me; if the vows that were paid to me pleased you but little, you had only to show yourself, to conceal no longer from men that perfect beauty which has but to show itself in order to bring them back to their duty.

Ven. You should have guarded better against these vows; this veneration, this incense ought to be declined, and in order to undeceive them more effectively, you should yourself have rendered this homage to me in their presence. You found pleasure in this error, from which on the contrary you should have shrunk with horror. Your haughty temper, proud of having rejected a thousand kings, has carried the extravagant ambition of its choice even to the skies.

Psy. Have I in my ambition aspired to heaven?

Ven. Your insolence is without an equal; do you not aspire to the gods when you reject all the kings of the world?

Psy. If Love had hardened my heart to all their passion, and had reserved me for himself alone, do I stand guilty? and must you to-day as a price for so dazzling a love crush me with everlasting sorrow?

VEN. Psyche, you should have known your position better, and the rank of this god.

PSY. And has he allowed me time and opportunity for doing so when from the first he became absolute master of my heart?

VEN. You have allowed your heart to be charmed by him, and you have loved him as soon as he said, "I love."

PSY. How could I refuse to love the god who inspires all with love, and who was pleading his own cause? He is your son; you well know his power, his merit.

VEN. Yes; he is my son; but a son who excites my wrath; a son who ill returns to me what he knows is due; a son who knows that I am forsaken, and who, the more to flatter his own unworthy affection, since you return his love, wounds no one, forces no one to come to my shrine and address his supplications to me. You have made a rebel of him; but the whole world shall behold my dire revenge on you, and I shall teach you whether it is meet for a mortal maiden to suffer a god to sigh at her feet. Follow me; you shall find by your own experience to what degree of mad self-reliance this ambition was leading you. Come, and arm yourself with as much patience as you possess presumption.

FOURTH INTERLUDE.

The scenes represent the infernal regions; a sea of fire is discovered, whose waves are rolling unceasingly. This terrible sea is enclosed by burning ruins; and, standing in the midst of the raging billows, through a frightful opening, appears PLUTO'S *palace. Eight* FURIES *issue from it, and form the entry of the ballet, in which they show their delight at having kindled such dire wrath in the heart of the sweetest of divinities. A* GOBLIN *adds perilous jumps to their dances, and meanwhile* PSYCHE, *who, in obedience to* VENUS, *has come to the infernal regions, is seen crossing again in* Charon's *bark, holding the box given to her by* PROSERPINA *for* VENUS.

ACT V.

SCENE I. — — PSYCHE (*alone*)

Alas! Ye awful waves of hell, ye gloomy palaces where Megaera and her sisters hold their court, far ever foes to the sun's light, amongst your Ixions and your Tantaluses, in the midst of so many incessant tortures, in these hideous recesses, what pain, what toil so great as those to which Venus condemns my love? Yet my troubles satisfy not her wrath; and since I am subject to her laws, since I see myself a prey to her resentment, in these cruel moments I must have had more than one soul, more than one life, to fulfil her commands. Yet all this I could bear with joy if, in the midst of her hatred, my eyes could behold, were it for one moment only, my darling, my beloved lover! His name I dare not utter; my lips, whose guilt it was to exact too much, are now unworthy of him; and in this deadly anguish, the keenest pain my ever-returning death subjects me to is that I may not see him. If his anger lasted still, no anguish could equal mine; but if he felt any pity for a soul that worships him, however great the sufferings to which I am condemned, I should feel them not. Yea, thou mighty destiny, if he would but stay his wrath, all my sorrows would be at an end. Ah! a mere look from the son suffices to make me insensible to the mother's fury. I will doubt it no longer; he shares my grief, he sees what I endure, and weeps with me; my sufferings are his too; it is a self-imposed law of love; in spite of Venus, in spite of my crime, he it is who sustains and revives me in the midst of the dangers I have to encounter. He harbours still the tender feelings urged by his passion, and hastens to restore me to new life as soon as I perish. But what would with me those two shades I see advancing towards me through the doubtful light of these dark recesses?

SCENE II. — —PSYCHE, CLEOMENES, AGENOR.

Psy. Cleomenes, Agenor, is it not you whom I see? Who has deprived you of life?

CLE. The meetest grief that could have caused a noble despair. That funeral pomp where you awaited the fiercest rigour and highest injustice of a fate most dark.

AGE. On that same rock where heaven in its wrath was promising to you, instead of a husband, a dragon who would forthwith devour you, we held ourselves ready to repulse his fury, or die with you. You know it well, Princess; and when you disappeared from our gaze through the air, both, equally carried away by our love and grief, cast ourselves headlong from that rock, in order to follow your beauty, or rather to feel that love-born joy of offering in your behalf a first prey to the monster.

CLE. We were fortunately deceived as to the meaning of your oracle; but here we have recognised its miracle, and learned that the serpent, ready to devour you, was the god who is the source of all love, and who, in spite of his divinity, adoring you himself, could not bear that mortals such as we are should presume to love you.

AGE. We now enjoy a pleasant death, as a reward for having followed you. What would have been life to us if we could not have been yours? Here we behold your charms once more; which neither of us would ever have seen again in the world above. Happy shall we be if we see the merest tear honour the misfortunes of which you have been the cause.

PSY. How can I have more tears to shed when my own misfortunes have been carried to the highest pitch? Let us mingle our sighs, since we have so fatal a destiny; we cannot exhaust sighs; but yours, Princes, are uttered in behalf of an ungrateful being. You would not survive my misfortune; but under whatever blow I fall, I cannot die for you.

CLE. Have we deserved aught else, we whose great passion has not ceased to weary you with the tale of our woes?

PSY. Princes, you might have won my whole soul but for your being rivals; those incomparable qualities which attended the vows of both rendered you too deserving of love to allow me to reject either.

AGE. You have been able, without injustice or cruelty, to refuse a heart reserved for a god. But behold Venus! Fate bids us return, and forces us to say "Farewell."

Psy. Is not leisure allowed you to tell me what your abode is here?

Cle. Among groves ever green, where we breathe naught but love; no sooner do we die of love than through love we revive; we sigh for love under the sweet laws of his blest empire; and everlasting night dares not expel from it the day which Love himself brings on our phantoms, which he inspires, and of which he forms a court even in Hades.

Age. Your envious sisters, who descended here below after us lost themselves in the hope of losing you. Both, each in turn, as a reward for the plot which cost them their life, suffer, now the rock at Ixion's side, now the vulture at Tityus'! Love, by means of the Zephyrs, has executed on them swift justice for their envenomed and jealous malice. Those winged ministers of his just wrath, under pretence of restoring them again to you, cast them both to the bottom of a precipice, where the hideous spectacle of their mangled bodies displays but the first and least torture for that stratagem the cunning of which was the cause of the ills you now endure.

Psy. How I pity them!

Cle. You alone are to be pitied; but we tarry too long conversing with you. Farewell! May we live in your remembrance; may you, and that soon, have nothing further to dread. Soon may Love exalt you to heaven, place you beside the other gods, and, kindling again a flame that cannot be extinguished, release for ever your beauteous eyes from the task of increasing daylight in these realms!

SCENE III.—— PSYCHE (*alone*).

Hapless lovers! their passion still continues; though dead, both love me—me, whose harshness so ill received their vows. 'Tis not thus thou actest—thou, who alone hast seized my heart; lover whom I still prize a thousand times more than my life, and who breakest such charming ties. Shun me no longer, and leave me to hope that one day thou shalt cast a glance on me, that by my sufferings, I shall please thee, and again win thy plighted faith. But my woes have disfigured me too much to allow to entertain such hopes. Eyes dejected, sad, despairing, pining, and with cheeks faded, what have I that can speak in my favour if some miracle impossible to foresee does not restore to me the beauty which once captivated thee? This treasure of divine beauty, which Proserpina has entrusted to me for Venus, contains charms which I can make mine own, and their lustre must be extreme, since beauty herself, Venus, requires them to adorn herself. Would it be a great crime to snatch a few? To captivate a god, who has been my lover, to recover his affection, and put an end to my torture, can anything that I may do be unlawful? Let me open it. What vapours cloud my brain? and what do I behold issuing from this open casket? Love, unless thy compassion forbids my death, I must needs descend to the tomb, never to live again.

PSYCHE *swoons, and* LOVE *flies towards her.*

SCENE IV.

LOVE. Thy danger, Psyche, dispels my wrath; nay, the violence of my passion has never abated; and though thou hast excited my highest displeasure, yet my anger was harboured only against my mother's wrath. I have seen all thy toils, I have followed all thy misfortunes, and throughout my sighs have answered thy tears. Look on me, I am still the same. What, again and again, I repeat that I love thee, and yet thou wilt not say that thou lovest me! Can it be that thy beauteous eyes are for ever closed, that they are for ever bereft of daylight? O Death! need'st thou have taken so cruel a dart, and, regardless of my eternal being, endangered my own life! How oft, ungrateful deity, have I swelled thy dark empire by the contempt or the cruelty of a fierce and proud fair one? How many faithful lovers, since I must confess it, have I, through irresistible raptures, sacrificed to thee? Go, I shall wound no more souls, I shall pierce no more hearts, but with darts dipped in the divine liquors that foster heaven's immortal passions. I shall hurl them no more but to make as many lovers as there are gods. As for thee, thou inexorable mother, who forcest her to bereave me of what I held dearest in this world, dread, in thy turn, the effects of my wrath. Thou wouldst sway my feelings, thou who art often swayed by my will; thou who wearest a heart as sensitive as that of mortals; thou enviest to mine the raptures of thine own! But in this same heart I shall plunge such darts as shall be followed by jealous sorrow. I shall crush thee by abasing ravishments, and ever choose as objects for thy dearest longings Adonises and Anchises who will nurse nothing but hatred towards thee.

SCENE V.— —VENUS, LOVE, PSYCHE (*still senseless*).

VEN. The threat is full of respect, and the anger of a rebellious son presumptuous….

LOVE. I am no longer a child; my childhood has been but too long, and my wrath is as just as it is impetuous.

VEN. Its impetuosity should be subdued, and thou oughtest to remember that to me thou owest thy birth.

LOVE. And thou mightest well not forget that thou possessest a heart and beauty that hold their power from me; that my bow is the only support of this power, that without my shafts it is nothing, and that if the stoutest hearts have suffered themselves to be drawn in thy triumphant train, thou hast never enslaved any one whose chains it was not my pleasure to forge. Mention no more those rights of birth that fetter my desires; and if thou dost not wish to lose a thousand sighs, pay thy tribute to gratitude when thou seest me; thou whose glory and delights are the offsprings of my power.

VEN. How hast thou defended this glory of which thou speakest? How hast thou restored it to me? And when thou hast seen my shrines deserted, my temples violated, the honours due to me rivalled by those of another, if thou hast shared my shame, how hast thou punished Psyche, who hath stolen them from me? I bade thee throw a spell over her, that she might love the basest of mortals, who would not condescend to answer her passion but by continual repulse and cruellest contempt; and thyself thou hast loved her! Thou hast seduced immortal deities against me; for the Zephyrs have concealed her from me; for thee, Apollo himself, by an oracle cleverly turned, had snatched her from my power so well that, but for the curiosity which by a blind distrust restored her to my vengeance, she escaped for ever my angry passion. See to what thy love has reduced her, thine own Psyche! See! her soul is even now departing; and if thine is still smitten, receive now her last breath. Threaten and brave me if thou wilt, but she must die. So much insolence suits thee well; and I must needs bow to all it pleases thee to say, I, who can do nothing without thy darts.

LOVE. Thy power is but too great, relentless goddess! Fate abandons her to thy wrath; but be less inexorable to the prayers and tears of a son who beseeches thee on his knees. It must be a pleasant sight enough for thee to see on one side Psyche expiring, on the other a son who, in a suppliant voice, wishes to hold his heart's happiness from thee only. Give me back my Psyche, restore to her all her charms, surrender her to my tears, to my love, to my grief; for she is my eyes' delight, my heart's happiness.

VEN. However deep thy love for Psyche, do not expect me to put an end to her misfortunes. If Fate abandons her to me, I abandon her to her fate. Importune me no more, and let her in the midst of her calamities triumph or perish without Venus.

LOVE. Alas! if I am too importunate, I would not be so if I could but die!

VEN. This grief is not common that drives an immortal to long for death.

LOVE. Thou mayest judge of the intensity of my passion by its very excess; wilt thou not be merciful?

VEN. I must confess thy love touches my heart; it disarms, it abates my sternness; thy Psyche shall see the light again.

LOVE. How powerfully I shall cause thy sway to be felt everywhere!

VEN. Ay! thou shalt behold her decked in her first beauty; but I will have the entire deference of thy grateful vows. I will that a true respect allow my love to select for thee another spouse.

LOVE. And I will have no such grace; I assume all my former boldness; I will have Psyche; I will have her plighted faith; I will that she live again, and that she live for me; and I reckon as naught that thy wearied hatred give way to favour another maiden. Jupiter, who even now appears, shall judge betwixt us, and decide between my insubordination and thy wrath.

The lightning flashes, the thunder rolls, and JUPITER *appears in the air borne aloft by his eagle.*

SCENE VI. — —JUPITER, VENUS, LOVE, PSYCHE (*senseless*).

LOVE. O thou to whom alone all is possible, father of gods, lord of mortals, soften the rigour of an inexorable mother, who without me would have no shrines. I have wept, I have supplicated; I sigh, I threaten. Sighs and threats are alike vain. She will not perceive that on my displeasure hangs the happy or sad condition of the whole world, and that if Psyche dies, if Psyche be not mine, I am no longer "Love". Yes! I shall break my bow, shatter my arrows; I shall even extinguish my sacred flame, and leave all nature to pine to death; or if I deign to wound a few more hearts with these golden shafts that arrest my sway, I shall wound you all above in behalf of mortals, while I shall hurl against them blunted darts only that inspire hatred, and produce thankless and cruel rebels. What tyrannical law is this that would bind me to keep my shafts ever ready to serve you, and would have me make conquest upon conquest for you, while you forbid me to make one for myself?

JUP. (*to* VENUS). My daughter, show thyself less severe towards him; his Psyche's destiny is even now in thy hands. Fate, at thy slightest word, is ready to follow up thy wrath. Speak, and let a mother's tenderness prevail upon thy designs. All dread this wrath which awes even me. Will thou leave the world to become the prey of hatred, disorder, and confusion, and change a god of union, of delights, of joy, into one of bitterness and division? Consider the lofty rank we hold, and say whether passion ought to sway our feelings. The word revenge is pleasing to mortals; the more is it meet that we should resort to forgiveness.

VEN. I forgive this rebel son. Yet would you have me submit to the reproach that a contemptible mortal, the object of my wrath, proud Psyche, because she displays some charms, has defiled my alliance and my son's couch?

JUP. Well, then, I make her immortal, so that all shall be equal.

VEN. I feel no longer hatred or contempt for her, but admit her to the honour of this conjugal tie. Psyche! recover your life, never more to lose it. Jupiter has contrived your restoration, and I abandon that lofty humour which opposed itself to your wishes.

PSY. (*recovering from her fainting condition*). It is you then, mighty goddess, who restores the life to this innocent being?

VEN. Jupiter extends his pardon to you, and my wrath lasts no longer. Live! Venus commands it. Love allows it.

PSY. (*to* LOVE). At last I see you again, dear object of my passion!

LOVE. (*to* PSYCHE). You are mine at last, my soul's own delight!

JUP. Come, lovers, come; and conclude in heaven so great, so lofty a union. Come, fair Psyche, to change thy destiny, and take thy place among the gods.